St. Helens Libraries

Please return / renew this item by the last date shown.
Books may be renewed by phone and Internet.

Telephone - (01744) 676954 or 677822
Email - centrallibrary@sthelens.gov.uk
Online - sthelens.gov.uk/librarycatalogue
Twitter - twitter.com/STHLibraries
Facebook - facebook.com/STHLibraries

- 5 JUL 2019

First published by Pugalugs Ltd in 2015

Written by Jessica Parish
Designed and illustrated by Helen Poole
Edited by Book Helpline

A CIP catalogue record for this book is available from the British Library.

ISBN 978-0-9930479-1-6

Printed and manufactured in China.

Pugalugs Ltd
The Enterprise Centre
Salisbury Street
St Helens
WA10 1FY
www.pugalugs.co.uk

The Adventures Of

Pugalugs™

Walkies

Written by
Jessica Parish

Illustrated by
Helen Poole

Have you ever been really excited about something? So excited, that it makes you want to jump up and down and run around like crazy? Well, this is how Pugalugs felt when he heard the word "walkies" for the first time! He was a three-month-old pug puppy who was very excited indeed.

Pugalugs knew exactly what "walkies" meant. He had been dreaming about it for ages: his very first walk! The time had finally come for him to step outside into the big, wide world.

He couldn't wait to get out there!

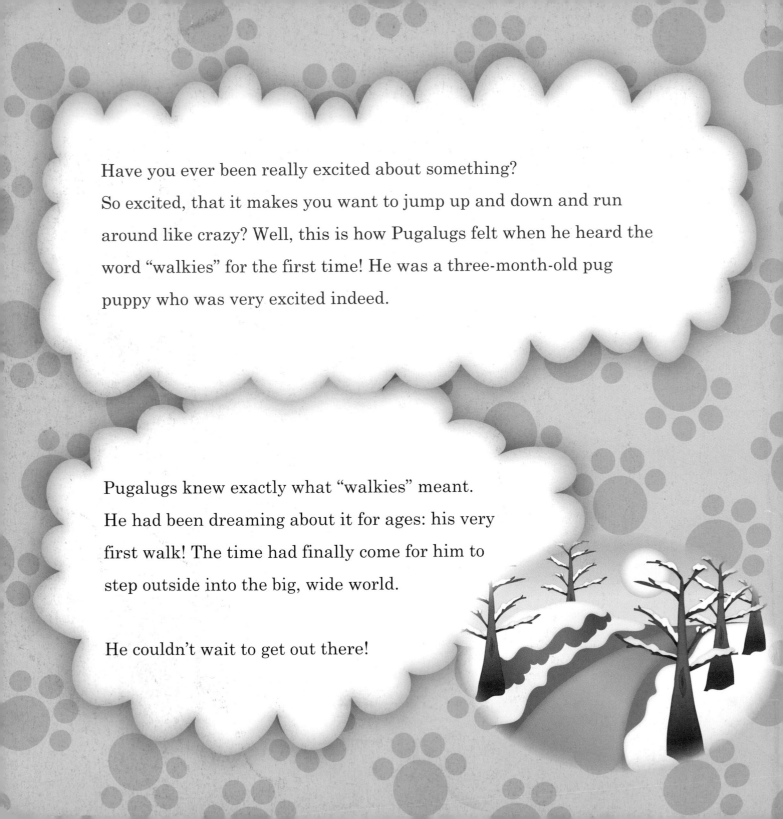

Pugalugs could see Connor walking towards him with a bright red, shiny lead and matching harness.

That was it, the excitement was too much. Pugalugs jumped up and down and ran around the kitchen table ten times!

"He's going bananas!" said Connor.

He laughed out loud as he watched his puppy scooting around the table as fast as lightening!

Pug puppies are full of energy and they need lots of exercise!

Connor had finally managed to catch Pugalugs and fastened him safely in his harness and lead. He was ready to go!

Pugalugs could only imagine what he might see on his first walk.
He was so glad that he had Connor to show him around. After all, Connor was ten years old, that's seventy in dog years. Surely he would know all the best things to see!

"It's very cold today, Pugalugs," said Connor, "but don't worry, you'll soon get used to it."

Pugalugs wasn't worried about being cold. He had his fur to keep him warm and toasty but he did wonder how he might look if he had to wear a woolly hat like Connor!

Just as they were about to reach the front door Pugalugs stopped.
He thought about Dug and Bella, his brother and sister. Weren't they
coming too? "Come on you two, it's time for walkies!" he called.

Dug and Bella were both curled up, half asleep in their bed.
"Snooze…" said Dug. "So comfy…" said Bella.

Pugalugs carried on towards the front door.
He would have to tell those two sleepyheads
all about his adventure when he
returned later.

It was nearly the end of winter but there was still a light covering of snow on the ground.

Connor opened the front door and Pugalugs bravely stepped outside.
He took a few tiny steps but then stopped. His paws were freezing!
He dug his feet into the ground and refused to walk any further.

Connor looked down at Pugalugs and gently tugged on his lead.
"Come on, Pugalugs!" he pleaded. "You won't feel the cold after a while."
Pugalugs looked up at Connor and tilted his head. He hoped that Connor was right.

Pugalugs thought about his cold, little paws, but suddenly he was distracted. He was sure that he could see his brother, Dug, just down the road. He was on a lead too, and he had turned into a giant!

Pugalugs leapt forward and tried to run towards Giant Dug.

"Whoa, slow down," laughed Connor, "I'm supposed to be the one walking you, not the other way around!" Pugalugs had to speak to Dug, and he had to find out how he had managed to get so big!

"Dug, it's me, Pugalugs!" he called out. The giant dog tilted his head at Pugalugs. He looked confused.

"I'm not Dug, I'm Bobby. Nice to meet you," said the dog.

"Bobby?" asked Pugalugs. "Are you a pug like me?"

"Nope, I'm a boxer dog," said Bobby.

"Wow," said Pugalugs, "a boxer dog! Wait till I tell the others!"

He looked at Bobby's tail. It was straight, not curly like his own.

Bobby could never be a pug with a tail like that!

After saying goodbye to Bobby, Pugalugs and Connor continued to walk. Pugalugs was really enjoying himself and he wasn't cold at all!

As they walked along the pathway, not far from their home, Pugalugs spotted a very strange little creature. It was hopping along on the grass next to them.

This animal had white fur, it was about half the size of Pugalugs and it had huge ears!

"Wow, you've sure got big ears for a pug!" said Pugalugs to the small animal.

"I'm not a pug, silly! I'm a rabbit. My name is Harriet, nice to meet you," she replied.

"Oh, I've never met a rabbit before!" said Pugalugs to Harriet. "How exciting!"

"What is your name?" asked Harriet.

"My name is Pugalugs. I'm out here on my very first walk!" he replied.

"Well, have fun," said Harriet. "I'd better be off now, see you!"

And with that, she sped off and disappeared into a hole in the ground.

Pugalugs and Connor carried on walking along the pathway.

He wondered what they would see next.

Suddenly, Pugalugs felt a breeze above his head. Something was flying above him.

Was it a helicopter, or an aeroplane? He was about to find out!

The flying object swooped right over Pugalugs' head. It came so close to him that it made the hairs on the back of his neck stand on end!

"Whoa there!" shrieked Pugalugs as he ducked his head.

"Sorry buddy," said the flying creature, "I didn't mean to scare you." Pugalugs peered up. "Wow, a pug with wings!" he cried. He couldn't believe what he was seeing.

"I'm not a pug, I'm a seagull. Sammy the seagull," the creature said.

Pugalugs stared up at Sammy in amazement. "See you around, little buddy," called Sammy as he flew off ahead.

Surely Pugalugs had seen everything now?

Pugalugs and Connor trotted along the pathway a little further. The sun was breaking through the clouds and Pugalugs was enjoying the warmth of the sun on his face. He was also enjoying all of the new smells in his nose! The outside world smelled very different from the inside of their home. It was so much more exciting being outside!

Pugalugs and Connor reached a wooden gate at the end of the pathway. Beyond the gate was an even longer pathway surrounded by trees. Connor didn't go through the gate, instead he turned around and they started to walk back towards home.

"One day, when you're a little older, we'll walk through the gate and all the way to the big lake in the middle of the woods!" said Connor to Pugalugs. "But now we better be heading home, it's nearly time for dinner."

Pugalugs walked along with a spring in his step, dinner time was his favourite time of day!

Lake - 1 mile

Please close
the gate!

Back they went towards home. Pugalugs wondered what he would be having for dinner that night. He hoped it would be his favourite: chicken-flavour puppy food and milk!

As they walked along, Pugalugs spotted a funny little creature. It was about the same size as he was and it sat on the grass next to them. It was black and white in colour. He had never seen anything like it before! It had a little face, pointy ears and huge whiskers! The creature stared at Pugalugs. He thought he had better introduce himself to this new friend.

Pugalugs pulled on his lead towards the little animal. "Hi, I'm Pugalugs the Pug. What's your name…?" He had barely reached the animal when it ran off in the opposite direction!

Pugalugs had never seen anything run so fast! He was confused. He looked up at Connor and tilted his head.

"Don't worry," said Connor, "that was Lucy, our neighbour's cat. She is a bit frightened of dogs when she first meets them. You'll probably see her again soon."

"Next time I see Lucy I'll be extra friendly!" thought Pugalugs, before his thoughts went back to his dinner.

Pugalugs and Connor stood waiting to cross over the road, which took them back to their street. They were nearly home and Pugalugs was hungry, his tummy was rumbling. He didn't realise that walking would give him such an appetite.

"Stay..." said Connor to Pugalugs. "Before we cross the road, we always have to look both ways, and check that there are no cars coming. We have to be very careful."

Pugalugs was a bit confused. He had never seen a car and he didn't know what Connor was talking about.
A few seconds later, a big blue box on wheels roared past them as they waited to cross! It was so fast, it made Pugalugs nearly jump out of his skin! There were two children sitting in the back who waved to Connor and he waved back at them.

"I guess that's a car," thought Pugalugs, "and they must be Connor's friends!" He imagined what it might be like if he had to ride in a car.

Pugalugs and Connor crossed the road safely and reached the other side. They were back on their own street now and were nearly home. It was starting to get dark outside and Pugalugs was getting tired. It would soon be time for him to curl up in bed and have a little puppy snooze! After all of the excitement of the day, Pugalugs knew that as soon as his head touched the soft, comfy bed, he would be fast asleep.

As he was daydreaming about his fluffy, warm bed, Pugalugs suddenly felt like he was falling. The pavement was gone from beneath his paw and his front leg had gone down a hole in the ground!

He panicked at first, but as he looked down he realised that he couldn't completely fall down the hole. It was too small, and he was on a lead after all.
"Oops, watch out for grids!" laughed Connor.
Pugalugs pulled his leg out of the grid and decided to walk around it this time!
He chuckled to himself at his near fall. He knew that Dug and Bella would love to hear this story!

Pugalugs and Connor walked back into the house. They were finally back at home and Pugalugs was very hungry and thirsty!

Connor took him out of his harness and Pugalugs ran quickly to the kitchen and straight to his food bowl. Waiting for him was a cold bowl of milk and some chicken puppy food. He was so happy to see his favourite meal in front of him. He ate the food within seconds and gulped down all of the milk.

After his dinner Pugalugs was a mess. He had food all over his face and his ears. He had been so excited to see his dinner that he had dived head first into the bowl to eat it all as quickly as he could!

"You're a mucky pup!" said Connor to Pugalugs as he cleaned his face and ears.

Once he was clean again, Pugalugs made his way over to his bed. Dug and Bella were curled up in bed already and Pugalugs jumped in with them.

"I've had the most amazing day," Pugalugs said to his brother and sister. "You will never believe what I have seen!" Dug and Bella listened intently, they wanted to know everything!

"First there was Bobby, the boxer dog. Then Harriet who lives in a hole, then Sammy who can fly! Oh, and you have to watch out for these tricky things called grids..."

"Wow" said Dug, "what else?" But Pugalugs had fallen fast asleep! Dug and Bella would have to wait until the morning to hear the rest of the story so they decided to go back to sleep themselves.

The three little pugs all began to snore as they dreamed about their next adventure.

To be continued...

Pugalugs

Dug

Bella

Connor

Bobby

Harriet

Sammy

Lucy

COMING SOON!

Look out for the next Pugalugs book!

The Adventures of Pugalugs: The Magic Bone!

Join Pugalugs, Dug and Bella on their next adventure

as they escape from their garden and find themselves

lost deep in the woods!

How will they find their way home?

Could a golden bone be the answer?

For news and updates visit:
www.pugalugs.co.uk